The Night of the Lights

Written and Illustrated by A. Elizabeth Orley

Edited by Penelope Walker-Quade

Dedicated to my sons Nolan & Zane

Love, Mom

2020© by A. Elizabeth Orley

 BooKS

ISBN 978-1-7350879-0-0 (ebook)
ISBN 978-1-7350879-2-4 (hardbound)
Printed in the United States of America

LIVE Publishing Company

LivePublishing Company

Gigi days were the best.

Every time Gigi would pick up Sam, they would have an entire day of

adventures together.

Today was one of those days. It felt like it took forever for this day to come.

Sam stood at the window waiting for Gigi's old blue truck.

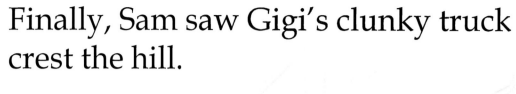

Finally, Sam saw Gigi's clunky truck crest the hill.

Sam leapt up and sang out in excitement, eager to see what adventure was waiting for them.

"Gigi, what took you so long?" Sam called out as Gigi pulled up to the curb.

"Nice to see you too, Sam," she said sarcastically.

The drive to Gigi's house was never too long, but the lines on the road couldn't sweep past the windows fast enough for Sam's liking.

Finally, they arrived.

Gigi's red door beckoned them inside,
with the lion knocker secured
in its center.

For Sam, Gigi's big red door opened
a magical world full of adventure.

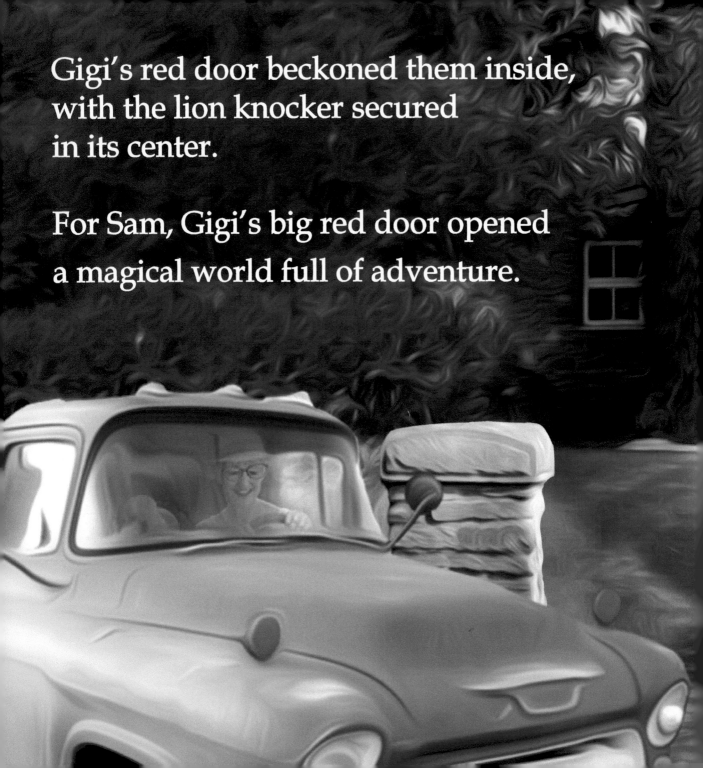

"I have something special planned for us today,"

said Gigi.

"Are we going to make rocket ships today, Gigi?"

"Oh no, Sam, rocket ships will have to wait."

"Are we going to paint today?"

"No, today we are going to enjoy one of nature's spectacular sights!"

They went through the old house and stepped into the backyard.

"I'll be right back Sam," said Gigi.

Gigi returned from the house with two jars and set them on the table.

"Today, as the sun goes down, we are going to sit on the porch and wait."

"Wait for what?" asked Sam.

"You will see,"

said Gigi, winking.

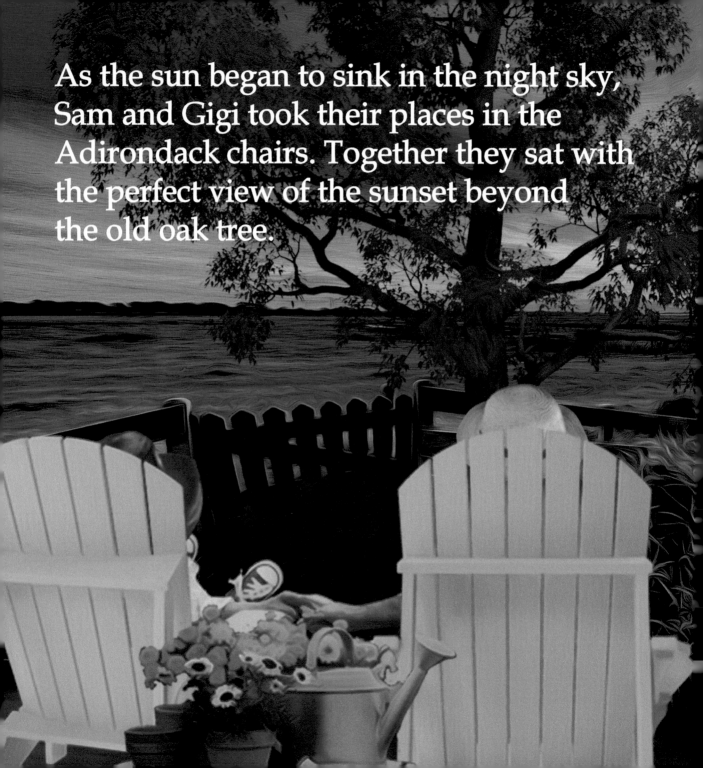

As the sun began to sink in the night sky, Sam and Gigi took their places in the Adirondack chairs. Together they sat with the perfect view of the sunset beyond the old oak tree.

The crickets began to chirp, and the sky went from blue, to yellow, to orange and purple.

"It's time..."

Sam observed that the stars in the city didn't shine as brightly as they did at Gigi's house. The city had so many different sounds and smells.

Gigi's house was different. It seemed calm, soft, and magical.

"Gigi, why are the stars so low?"

"The stars are firmly planted in the sky, my love. What you are seeing is not the stars,"

Gigi said mysteriously.

Sam had never seen such beautiful dancing lights in the city. The city was filled with many lights at night, but nothing so small and magical.

"Tonight, we are going to catch fireflies."

Gigi whispered, gazing out at the twinkling lights that now filled the sky.

Gigi handed Sam one of the jars and said,

"You have to focus on just one light until you get one in the jar"

Then she removed the jar's lid, and set it back on the table.

"Fireflies appear and disappear, and you have to follow them to catch them," Gigi explained.

"What fun!" Sam exclaimed before setting out into the yard to begin the adventure.

Sam was getting the hang of catching fireflies.
After a few failed attempts, Sam quickly
moved the jar into the path of a firefly.

Sam tried to put a hand over the jar.
After flickering away,

on-off-on-off

the little firefly
escaped through the
cracks of Sam's fingers.

As the little beetle flew
away it seemed to say,

"Goodbye,"

disappearing into
the stars above.

Sam noticed many more little flickers of light. This time, Sam carefully captured a pair of little friends who seemed to blink together,

on-off-on-off.

Realizing it would take two hands to completely cover the top of the jar, Sam knew there would be no way to cover and carry it at the same time.

Sam needed some sort of lid to keep the new little friends contained in the jar.

But where was the lid?

Sam remembered that Gigi had taken the lid off, before handing over the jar.

Sam needed to think.

The light from the moon was bright enough to see some of Gigi's garden tools lying about.

After a quick survey, Sam saw a trowel, hoe, snippers, and a pair of garden gloves.

The tools with the long handles and heavy ends would not work to cover the mouth of the jar.

What else, what else?

The gloves!

The opening to Gigi's garden gloves fit
perfectly over the mouth of the jar.

Once Sam covered the jar, the little
beetles were able to move with ease,
and they glowed even brighter as if to
approve of their new environment.

Sam gazed at them, marveling
at the flashing little lights.

Soon, Gigi called Sam back to the porch.

"Gigi, I caught one!" Sam exclaimed." But then it escaped. Then I caught two more, but I needed to borrow something of yours to keep them inside."

"Anything of mine is yours, Sam. What did you need?"

"Well," said Sam shyly,
"you forgot to give me the LID!"

Then Sam lifted the jar to show her
how the floppy glove worked
as the perfect substitute.

"Oh my," said Gigi,

"I see you found a
creative alternative Sam! "

Sam beamed with wonder at the fireflies twinkling inside the jar.

Then Sam said with excitement,

"Gigi, can we keep them?"

"If we keep the fireflies in the jar, they will be lonely, and they won't flicker anymore. But if we set them free, they will go back to their friends and light up the night again for us for many more visits," said Gigi.

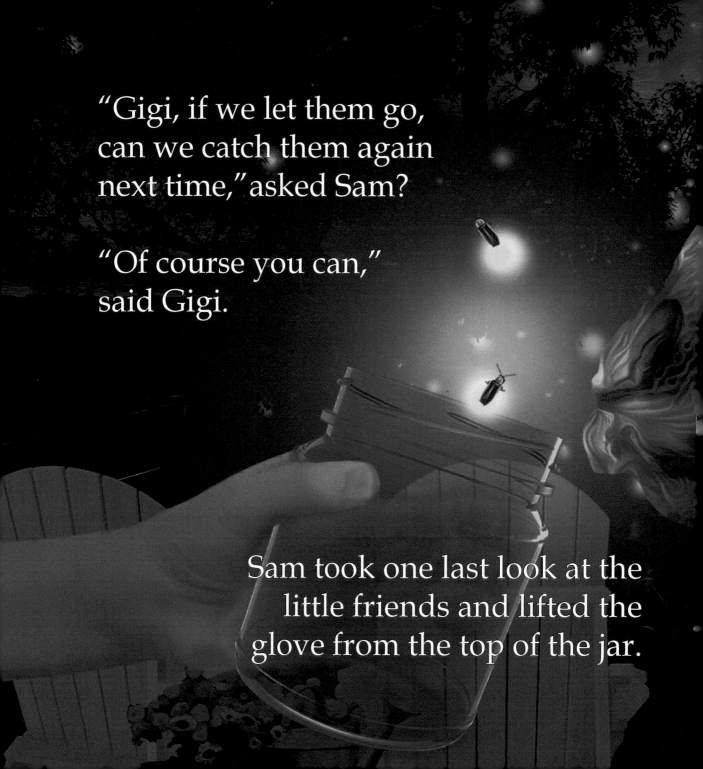

"Gigi, if we let them go,
can we catch them again
next time," asked Sam?

"Of course you can,"
said Gigi.

Sam took one last look at the
little friends and lifted the
glove from the top of the jar.

"Go free, my little friends."

Sam's eyes lit up as the fireflies flickered again in the night sky.

"Bye, friends," said Sam a little tearfully.

"Oh Sam, come here and give me a hug. We can do this again soon," said Gigi.

"And next time, I will remember to give you the lid!" she said as she wrapped her arms around Sam.

The end

Firefly Fun Facts

Fireflies are one of the species that are bioluminescent, which means that they can create their own light.

The light of a firefly can be yellow, green, or orange.

There are more than 2,000 species of fireflies in the world.

Fireflies are actually a type of beetle.

Fireflies are now on the endangered species list.

To help save the fireflies, check out

www.firefly.org